Misconduct

Deal with it without bending the rules

Anne Marie Aikins • Illustrated by Steven Murray

James Lorimer & Company Ltd., Publishers
Toronto

“Let’s go downtown!”

You’re on the sidewalk, and your best buddy is holding the back door of the bus open for you.

You don't have the fare, so why don't you just hop on board? Maybe because you know it would be breaking the rules. No matter what you want to do, it seems there are rules about how you should or should not behave.

Rules can seem like bad news for kids.

Rules are everywhere — at school, at home, at the mall, on the soccer field, and even on the street. From the strictest of laws to those things that everyone just assumes you should know, everywhere you look there are guidelines and limits to your conduct. Following them all sometimes seems impossible! But can you imagine a classroom or a home where no one followed the rules? Or how dangerous it might be if sports had no rules? In hockey, a player who breaks the rules can receive a type of penalty called a "game misconduct," which means they're off the ice for the rest of the game. The whole team pays for one player's mistake.

Almost everyone has broken a rule at one time or another. No matter how stupid a rule may seem, there is almost always a reason for it.

You may not see the harm in breaking a rule, but it always pays to stop and think. The choice is yours and you must decide if you're going to respect the rule or face the consequences of breaking it. If you're having trouble seeing where your conduct becomes misconduct, this book will help you understand how sometimes the rules, well ... rule!

Contents

What is misconduct?

punch someone's lights out

Everyone knows what misconduct is, right? It's when you break the rules. But how do you know the rules you have to follow? You know you shouldn't:

cheat on a school exam

play in restricted areas

jaywalk

break curfew

disobey traffic laws

litter

Sure, those rules are pretty clear. But sometimes it's harder to tell if you're breaking the rules. What about:

not paying the bills on time?

keeping something of value that you found?

not helping a person in need?

not listening to someone speak?

giving attitude?

skipping out on your chores?

swearing at your mother?

Whether clear and known by everyone — or not — rules are often what separates doing the right thing from doing the wrong thing.

Misconduct 101

Rules are in place to

Quick, let's get outta here.
EXIT
I think you guys forgot to pay for something.
oh no!

uphold . . .

Yeah, yeah, Mom...
SHE SNEAKS OUT LATER WITHOUT DOING THE DISHES.
See ya later.
That girl is so grounded!

SHE CHATS WITH A BOY AND AGREES TO MEET HIM LATER.
Christine says: (9:30:22 AM)
OK, I'll see you downtown in front of the arcade!
AN OLDER MAN IS WAITING FOR CHRISTINE AT THE ARCADE.
Girl Attacked by Internet Stalker

Hey, we've been in line for half an hour!
Outta my way, shrimps.
We'll give your money back, but you have to leave.

Misconduct 101

QUIZ

So, there are usually good reasons for rules, and breaking a rule has consequences. But sometimes what we call a rule is more like a guideline, and it's up to you to make up your mind whether or not to follow it. Decide whether each of the following situations shows a rule that should be followed or a personal choice. Check your answers on the following page.

1 Breakfast Battle

Brad's mom insists he eat a balanced healthy diet. Brad hates the oatmeal she makes for breakfast, so every morning he eats fruit and toast.

2 Outfit Outrage

Jenny sneaks out of the house wearing a really short skirt and a top that shows her belly. It's an outfit her mom told her not to wear.

3 For Pete's Sake

Matthew doesn't like his name. He tells people his name is Pete and only answers to that name.

4 Don't Do Dancing

Phuong is shy and refuses to go to school dances. He even stays in the classroom and reads while the rest of his class is given time to make decorations for the next dance.

5 Lazy Reader

Frankie does his book report without reading the whole book. His teacher gives him a B.

6 Text Off!

Ryan and Mandy are close friends who like to pass notes and secretly text-message each other in class.

7 Extreme Exteriors

Jasmine often wears pretty far-out clothes with weird accessories when she goes out with her friends.

8 Teasing Trio

A group of boys at school are always teasing the younger kids. They say it's just in fun.

9 Excess Baggage

Every time Kareem goes into his favourite music store, the clerks ask him to leave his bag at the counter. It makes him angry, but he always complies.

10 Musical Moments

Julie likes her music loud and keeps her headphones on all the time.

Answers

1. As long as Brad eats a balanced diet, it's his choice to decide what he eats for breakfast.
2. Jenny's mom doesn't want her to look inappropriate or too old for her age. There are lots of fashion choices Jenny can make that would fit within her mom's rules.
3. Even if it bugs everyone, it's Matthew's (or Pete's) choice what name he's called.
4. It's Phuong's choice whether or not he participates in social activities. But it might be a good idea for him to talk to someone about why he's so shy.
5. Taking a shortcut through his homework is still cheating and breaking the rules, even if the teacher doesn't find out.
6. If the classroom rule is no chatting, these students are breaking it. Text-messaging and passing notes creates the same distraction as talking.
7. Unique styles are personal choices. And as long as her parents give her the freedom to choose her own clothes, Jasmine isn't breaking a rule.
8. Teasing, especially when done in groups, is bullying. And any kind of bullying is against schoolyard rules.
9. It may be the store's policy that customers must check their bags. If not, Kareem should find out why he is being singled out for special — and unfair — treatment.
10. Unless Julie wears the headphones someplace she's been told not to — like in class — it's her choice to listen as often as she likes. She should make sure she's not disturbing others, though.

Dear Conduct Counsellor

Q: I really love the thrill it gives me when I ride my bike down this big hill, nearly missing the train as it passes. Isn't it my business if I want to take risks?

— Risk-Taker

A: It sounds like you like to have fun, but many rules are there to keep you safe and to protect other people or things. Someone could get hurt if you collided with the train or if the train attempted to stop quickly to avoid you. You may even be breaking the law. There are safer ways to get thrills, like riding a rollercoaster or racing on a bike track. And there are lots of other ways you can use your courageous and bold spirit to have fun without risking your life or the safety of others.

Q: I understand the rules when they are explained, but I get really confused about the ones that aren't written down. My guardian says I'm supposed to be polite to grown-ups, but why does anyone care if I'm rude to a stranger?

— Talking (Back) to Strangers

A: You're not alone. Lots of people have trouble with the unspoken rules, the ones about manners and courtesies. It's tough to follow a rule when you don't see the results of breaking it. But think about this: how you treat others, including people you don't know, tells others what kind of person you are.

Q: My parents overreact every time I make a mistake, and the punishments never fit my crimes. It makes me want to break the rules even more, and then I get more punishments. How do I handle the unfairness?

— Vicious Circle

A: Sometimes adults try to encourage kids to follow the rules by coming down really hard when they make mistakes. They want to help you learn because they think you will be better off in the long run. But there needs to be communication between you and the rule makers. By continually breaking the rules, you're just creating more trouble. Talk to your parents. Sometimes written "contracts" help families to negotiate fair rules and realistic consequences.

Q: Some rules are just stupid and others are really unfair. I have rights, so why should I obey rules like that. Shouldn't I stand up for myself?

— Rebel with a Cause

A: It's great that you want to stand up for yourself. But you might be missing the point of some of the rules you don't like. It's important to figure out why a rule is there and who or what it is designed to protect. If you do decide that a rule is wrong, there is a way to challenge it without creating big trouble for yourself. Speak with your guidance counsellor, team leader, or another adult to help you develop a strategy. As for your rights, remember that human rights are protected by law and a law is a type of rule!

Q: My older brother has always lived on the edge. He likes to cut corners so he has more time to have fun. His attitude has gotten him into trouble, and he didn't get into the college he wanted. But he's a great guy and, for the most part, he's done okay without following all the rules. So why should I?

— Following in his Footsteps

A: Sometimes when we see people we admire breaking the rules, it can be really tempting to follow their lead. But do you really want to risk your future just to have a little more fun? It might be that you don't know the whole story — did he let you see how upset he was when he didn't get admitted to the school of his choice? Your brother has gotten lucky getting away with breaking the rules, but that's his life, not yours. You must decide what's best for you, and be your own person.

Myths

Rules are made to be broken.

It's true that most rules are broken at some time by someone. But rules were created to help maintain order or to protect people or property, so breaking them puts these things at risk.

It doesn't matter if I just bend the rules.

Bending a rule is like bending a potato chip — it's impossible to do without breaking it.

Once a rule, always a rule.

Times change, and rules can be changed as circumstances change.

DID YOU KNOW?

- Many rules can be negotiated.
- People have more interest in following rules they help create.

If a rule is unfair or doesn't make any sense, it should be **broken.**

The reason behind a rule isn't always obvious. Take time to explore why a rule is there before you take action.

If a rule isn't **written down,** I don't have to follow it.

You're right, many rules come down to personal choice. And with all rules, it's ultimately up to you to decide. But there will still be consequences for breaking them.

If no one knows I broke a rule, then it **doesn't hurt anyone.**

You know you broke the rule. If you get away with breaking a rule, it may become easier for you to keep breaking other rules, and that's a hard habit to break.

- Every sport or game is made up of rules.
- Breaking rules can lead to more and more misconduct.
- 2/3 of Canadian youths charged with a crime have a history of breaking rules.

It seems like you're always in trouble.

If there's a rule, you'll break it. You're constantly getting punished for your misconduct.

You are a troublemaker.

So what's up with that? What do you get when you break the rules?

- You only have to think about yourself.
- You get to be your own boss.
- People may see you as brave and free-spirited.
- It can be fun.
- People notice you.
- Sometimes it gets you out of class.
- You get to do whatever you like.
- You don't have to be patient or thoughtful.
- You get to take whatever you want.
- You get to challenge injustices.

Being a troublemaker can be a good thing — it means you are bold and brave. Throughout history, people have challenged injustices and helped build a fairer society. And everyone breaks rules sometimes. Even adults.

But sometimes you break rules just to get back at someone or just to avoid responsibility. So your courageous, rebellious nature leads to trouble instead of positive change.

do's and don'ts

✓ Do realize you don't have to be perfect. Everyone makes mistakes.

✓ Do speak to your parents or another trustworthy adult about how you feel about having to follow the rules.

✓ Do believe it's never too late to change.

✓ Do try to adjust your attitude about rules.

✓ Do practise self-control.

✓ Do open your mind to the possibility of negotiating rules with your parents or teachers.

✓ Do try to avoid people who break the rules.

✓ Do use your courage to challenge injustices rather than breaking rules for its own sake.

✗ Don't automatically break a rule just because you can.

✗ Don't let getting into trouble become a habit.

✗ Don't hate the world and yourself.

✗ Don't try to solve the problem all by yourself. Get help.

✗ Don't give up.

QUIZ

How do you handle rules that are unfair?

Do you speak your mind? Or do you give in to misconduct and just break them all? There are two basic ways not to obey rules you think are unfair — aggressively or assertively. Acting aggressively may just get you into trouble. But if you behave assertively, you can help create rules that you're more likely to follow. Take this quiz and then check out your behaviour on the next page.

1 Curfew Feud

Your mom always makes you come home a lot earlier than the other kids. It makes you mad that she treats you like such a baby. Do you:
a) Just ignore her curfews?
b) Speak to your mom about a more reasonable time to come home from each event?

2 TEST TEMPTATION

You are flunking math because you just don't get the work. Someone in your class offers to give you a copy of the math exam. Do you: a) Say "no thanks," but ask your teacher for extra help to prepare? b) Take the exam so you can ace it?

3 FINDERS KEEPERS

You find a wallet full of money in the mall washroom. No one knows you found it. Do you: a) Take it — after all, who's going to know? b) Consider that there might be a reward and turn the wallet in to the lost and found?

4 BETTER SAFE THAN SORRY

Jabari wants to celebrate the holidays with fireworks. The man at the store says that only adults can purchase the fireworks. Should he: a) Ask his parents if they can have a block party to light off some fireworks? b) Pay an older friend to buy some fireworks and get his pals together to set them off in the local park?

5 SEAT SAVER

When Devon gets on the bus, the only seat available is one marked for the elderly and disabled, so he sits down. Two stops later, a woman with a cane gets on. There are empty seats nearer the door. Should he:
a) Tell the woman to take one of the other seats. b) Ask the woman if she wants his seat or one nearer the door?

6 Boys Rule

Kelly feels like she has more chores to do than her brothers. She gets stuck doing everything while the boys get to play video games. It's just not fair. Should she: a) Speak to her parents and discuss a fairer system of sharing the household tasks? b) Refuse to do her chores and blame her brothers?

7 Dress for Success

The new principal at Theresa's school has changed the dress code — no caps, sport jerseys, or belly tops. Should she: a) Wear whatever she feels like because the new rules are unreasonable? b) Ask her guidance counsellor to help her understand the new rules and develop a strategy to negotiate a more flexible dress code?

8 Taken for a Ride

Tyrone missed the last bus home and now he's going to miss curfew. Some guy he doesn't know pulls up in his car and offers him a ride home. Should he: a) Call home for a ride and arrange a back-up plan for next time? b) Take the ride from the stranger and hope for the best?

Answers

1. a) Aggressive	5. a) Aggressive	9. a) Assertive
b) Assertive	b) Assertive	b) Aggressive
2. a) Assertive	6. a) Assertive	10. a) Aggressive
b) Aggressive	b) Aggressive	b) Assertive
3. a) Aggressive	7. a) Aggressive	
b) Assertive	b) Assertive	
4. a) Assertive	8. a) Assertive	
b) Aggressive	b) Aggressive	

9 Shhh...

Fadi and Jan are watching a hilarious movie at the theatre. They're laughing really loud, and the people behind them complain to the management. Should they: a) Ask if they can change to a different theatre? b) Tell the usher to shut up and keep right on laughing at the movie they paid for?

10 Skating Turf

The neighbourhood kids have no place to skateboard anymore. The city has posted a "no skateboarding" sign in the local park. Should they: a) Continue skateboarding in the park? b) Ask their parents to help them talk to the city officials about finding another place for kids to skateboard?

Managing Misconduct

There are some basic things you can do to help you control your rebellious nature and keep it from getting you into trouble.

But, if you've gotten into the habit of talking back instead of negotiating fair rules, you need to practise these suggestions:

Explore Your Feelings

How does it make you feel when you are forced to follow an unfair rule — does it make you feel powerless? How do you feel when you break a rule — does it make you feel important, powerful, and brave? Think about the times you get into trouble. Be really honest with yourself about the mistakes you've made. Take responsibility.

Review the Rules

Are there particular types of rules that are the most troublesome for you? Or is it the people — like your parents or strangers — who make a rule that you have trouble with? You might be acting out against individuals rather than the rules themselves.

Examine the Consequences

How much trouble have you gotten into for breaking the rules? Is it worth it? It might be helpful for you to discuss this with a trusted adult like a guidance counsellor.

Find Fun Alternatives

It's part of your personality to want to be different and unique. That's good, except when it gets you into trouble. But it's people like you who create great things in this world. There are lots of safe ways you can show off your willingness to be different and to take risks. Spend time figuring out ways that would work for you. Learn to compromise.

DID YOU KNOW?

- Youths are charged most often with crimes such as mischief, disturbing the peace and minor thefts.

When Laws are Involved

Laws are like other rules taken up a notch. Obeying them is mandatory, and breaking them carries penalties. Sometimes laws exist to protect people and institutions from being sued. Many laws are in place to keep people from getting hurt.

Governments set laws and establish consequences for breaking them to encourage people to follow crucial rules. The police are responsible for enforcing the laws. A judge or a jury decides whether a person is guilty of breaking the law and what the punishment must be: a warning, a fine, or even jail time. Here are some examples of broken laws:

- Not wearing a helmet when riding a bicycle
- Driving a car without a valid driver's licence
- Drinking or smoking underage
- Physically harming a person or animal
- Stealing or shoplifting
- Destroying someone's property

If you witness a law being broken, you have a responsibility as a good citizen to do something. This isn't being a tattle-tale — your motivation is not just to get someone into trouble. Being a good citizen means taking responsibility to protect someone or something from harm.

Sometimes, when laws are very old, they become unfair in a modern world. You can challenge injustices by:

- Educating yourself about the history of the law
- Finding out what the law was designed to accomplish and why it is now outdated
- Looking into what is being done to challenge the law and seeking out groups that are working for change
- Using your voice at city hall or other government offices
- Attending rallies or protests
- Writing protest letters or e-mails, or signing petitions

Be a Leader

Sometimes rules are unfair or are designed without much thought, and sometimes the consequences don't fit the crimes. But there are ways to handle situations like this without creating trouble for yourself. Speak to your parents, older siblings, teachers, or a guidance counsellor. Speak up about the things that are bothering you and learn the skill of negotiating. If your misconduct has given you a reputation as a troublemaker, you may have to make lots of repairs, such as writing contracts with your parents, to get past it.

- Adults who have gotten into conflicts with the law often report that they had trouble following rules when they were young.
- In 2003, 84,000 youths aged 12–17 were charged with a criminal offence.

Are you terrified of getting into trouble?

Do you spend half your life trying to determine what the rules are so you don't break them? Do you get teased for being a goody two-shoes?
All your life, you've been told that you should follow the rules. It's scary making choices, so you'd prefer to take the safe route. You never question or try to negotiate a change in a rule.
So what's so bad about being a follower? It's a problem if following the rules all the time makes you feel powerless and angry. It's a problem if you follow rules you know are unfair.

Rules seem to be causing you a lot of trouble, too.

DEAR DR. SHRINK-WRAPPED . . .

Q: I am a very cautious person who always follows all the rules, no matter what. It frightens me when I see other kids breaking rules. I also have trouble making choices, and find it's easier just to follow along. Is there anything wrong with this?

— Scaredy-Cat

A: You have to remember that you always have a choice. You can be meek as a kitten and choose to go along with every rule, even when it's unfair. Or you can choose to be a lion, a rebel who respects the rules but challenges injustices. The good news is that you can start exercising your right to choose your conduct at any time, and you can learn to make good choices:

- Think about your personal goals. Ask yourself if the choice fits within those goals.
- Examine both the good and the bad consequences of the choice. Are the consequences worth it?
- Speak with a trusted adult. Ask them about their experiences. Explore all your options.
- Do the research. Find out what your real choices are and make an informed one.
- Look at the choices made by your role models. How did their choices lead them to success or failure?
- Don't make your choice in haste if you have time.
- If you make the wrong choice, admit you made a mistake and accept the consequences.

Q: I have lost friends in the past because they broke the rules and I didn't want to be around them. Now I'm starting at a new school. I've made some new friends, and don't want to lose these ones too. What should I do if I see my new friends getting into trouble?

— New Kid on the Block

A: Dr. Shrink-Wrapped thinks you are really trying to do the right things to keep yourself out of trouble. But that shouldn't mean that you end up without buddies! When your friends break the rules, there are ways to deal with the situation without being confrontational:

- Suggest to your friends that you all do something else instead.
- Remind them of the consequences.
- Tell them you don't feel like doing it.
- Tell them that getting into trouble is a terrible way for you to start at a new school.
- Negotiate a compromise.
- Suggest a better idea.
- Say that you don't have to run risks to have fun.
- Walk away.
- Excuse yourself and go to the bathroom.
- Say that you need to go home.
- If safety is an issue, get help.

QUIZ

Pushover or law-abiding citizen?

How do you usually respond to rules and limits? Take this quiz to find out if take following the rules more seriously than doing the right thing. How many of these statements are true about you?

1. I am never chosen to be in leadership positions.
2. I don't like taking risks.
3. My friends think I'm too timid.
4. Sometimes I get very nervous.
5. I don't like challenging authority.
6. I don't like making decisions.
7. I get confused when given too many choices.
8. People have told me I am not very open-minded.
9. I have never challenged a rule.

I don't like being different. 10

I don't like confrontation. 11

I don't like making mistakes. 12

Change is hard for me. 13

Admitting mistakes is hard for me. 14

My family overreacts when mistakes are made. 15

I think people are bad when they break rules. 16

I've been called a perfectionist. 17

I worry all the time about doing the right thing. 18

I can be very hard on myself. 19

Troublemakers scare me. 20

Did you score a lot of Trues? Maybe it's time to take a hard look at some of the rules you follow, and talk to someone about your fear of making mistakes.

The **Follower**

How can you deal with all the rules in your life without worrying so much about making mistakes?

Everyone makes mistakes — that's how we learn. There are many things you can do to make yourself more comfortable with rules and choices.

Examine your own behaviour and attitude about rules and limits. Open your mind to change. Believe it or not, rules are not purposely created to cause you trouble. They are usually there for good reasons, such as to promote safety and to help kids become responsible, compassionate, and educated adults.

Being well-behaved is a good quality, but leadership skills are great, too. Find an issue that is meaningful to you and work for change, like joining a human-rights organization. Take one step at a time towards becoming more comfortable with challenging some rules. You don't have to be perfect or change overnight. Remember, rules don't have to rule your world.

Use your determination to help develop fair rules in your school, ones that are well understood and accepted. Figure out what the rules are designed to accomplish. Negotiate appropriate rewards when rules are followed. And discuss fair consequences that help students learn from their mistakes.

Get involved in developing Good Choices clubs in your school or class. Led by a peer leader or guidance counsellor, these clubs provide an opportunity for kids to talk about misconduct in a

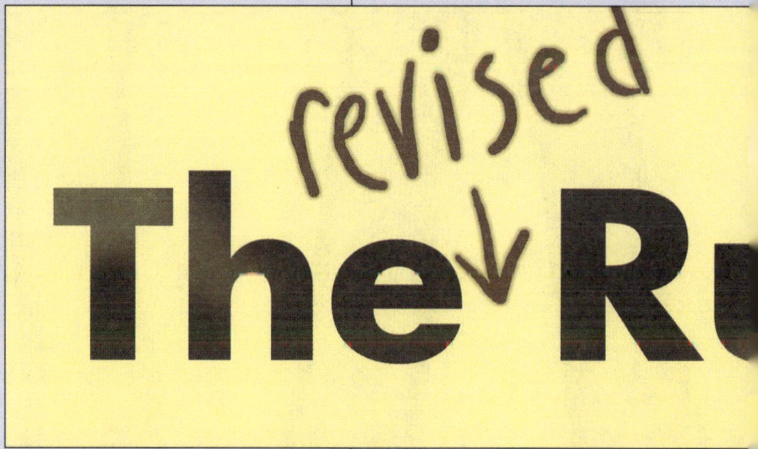

Did You Know?

- Also in 2003, 100,000 youths were involved in breaking laws, but not charged.

safe environment. Everyone can share their experiences and develop strategies to help them make good choices.

Talk to your family about ways they can help you develop a sense of responsibility. Remember, parents and guardians are learning to see you as an independent person. It may be scary for them to think about you making mistakes that could hurt you or your future. Try to understand their fears, and look for choice opportunities to earn their trust!

les

do's and don'ts

✓ Do educate yourself about rules.

✓ Do think about your choices.

✓ Do look for ways to challenge unfair rules.

✓ Do act responsibly.

✓ Do work on developing good decision-making skills.

✓ Do use your determination.

✓ Do work on improving your comfort level with new ideas.

✓ Do relax and try not to put so much pressure on yourself.

✗ Don't worry so much.

✗ Don't be judgmental.

✗ Don't be afraid of change.

✗ Don't panic if you make a mistake.

✗ Don't give up.

- Often people break rules because they don't understand why the rule is in place.
- More than half of young Internet users report they engage in risky behaviour because there aren't any house rules.

Were you ever around when someone broke a rule?

Have you witnessed a crime?

Think about what you did in that situation. Did you speak up or follow along? Maybe you told the person breaking the rule that you didn't think it was a good idea. Or maybe you found someone in charge to tell. Maybe you did nothing at all.

You do have a choice when you witness rules being broken.

Part of the Problem

Some witnesses don't know what to do or where to turn to for help. They become part of the problem by:

- being silent
- doing nothing when someone might get hurt
- accepting the benefits of misconduct, like eating stolen candy someone gives them
- admiring a person who breaks a rule
- pretending they are also breaking the rule

Not My Concern

Often people don't recognize or react when subtle rules are broken because there may appear to be few consequences. But there is always a consequence, even if we don't see it. And witnesses may also face the consequences when rules are broken. By speaking up or taking a stand, witnesses may fear they will:

- lose friends
- look like a coward
- interfere in something that's none of their business
- make a mistake
- misinterpret a person's intentions
- get someone in trouble

But someone might get hurt … or worse.

do's and don'ts

✓ Do educate yourself about rules.

✓ Do learn about choices.

✓ Do speak up. Get involved. Be a good citizen.

✓ Do talk to a trustworthy adult.

✓ Do get help — a teacher, supervisor, principal, neighbour, parent, or older friend.

✓ Do set a good example for others.

✓ Do treat everyone with respect.

✓ Do challenge rule breakers.

✗ Don't stand by and do nothing.

✗ Don't follow risky examples.

✗ Don't give up trying. Change happens one person at a time.

✗ Don't encourage rule breakers with your admiration.

QUIZ

Do you really understand misconduct?

Okay, so you think you understand the rules and what happens when they are broken. But do you really get it? What would you do in the following situations? This quiz has no right or wrong answers, because each situation is unique. Your answers may be different from the ones given below, but they could be right under the circumstance.

1 Babysitting Blues

Your friend asks you to come and study with her at her babysitting job for the evening, even though the parents told her she is not allowed to have any friends over. The project you're doing together is due tomorrow. What should you do?

- Ask your teacher for an extension on your project, and next time get the work done sooner.
- Suggest that your friend speak with the parents to see if there is any exception to the rule, and negotiate a reasonable time to go over.
- Schedule some time to work on your project before she has to babysit.

Breaking the rule may result in your friend losing the trust of the parents, and she may lose the job.

2 Promises, Promises

Garrick promised that he would help an elderly woman in his neighbourhood by cutting her grass. But your dad gave you a couple of tickets for an NHL game, and you want Garrick to go with you. He's willing to forget his promise.

- Take Garrick to the game. It's his decision.
- Suggest your friend speak with the neighbour and figure out a different time to cut the grass.
- Help your friend do the work before the game.

3 Jump Up

Your pals are all planning to go swimming at the water pits near the hydro towers just outside of town. They would be trespassing, but it's a really cool place to hang out.

- Decide not to go, but let them make their own decision.
- Talk to your friends about their choice. Suggest a safer place to hang out.
- Tell them about the consequences, such as getting into trouble with the police and their parents, as well as the safety risks.

4 G-Ball not B-Ball

Your best friend Francine wants to play basketball, but there are no girls' teams at your school and the boys' team doesn't allow girls to play. Francine boos the boys' team when it plays, and has vandalized the boys' locker room during a game.

- Talk to Francine about less destructive ways of approaching the rules.
- Ask the school administration for an explanation of the policy. State your thoughts about the discrimination clearly and politely. Try offering an option, like mixed teams.
- Explore other options in the community. There may be other leagues that Francine could play in.
- Get your parents' guidance, if necessary.

5 Butt Out

Your friend Jason is a smoker. You know it's bad for his health, and that his parents will freak out if they find out. You know that nagging or threatening Jason won't work. Is there anything you can do?

- Give Jason pamphlets on smoking to help him understand how addictive and deadly his new habit is and how difficult it will be to stop the longer he continues.
- Set up your own personal boundaries or rules on smoking — for example, no smoking around you — which might encourage Jason to stop.
- Remind Jason that it is illegal for stores to sell him cigarettes, and ask what kind of rules and laws he is breaking to get the cigarettes he smokes.

Continues . . .

6 TV TROUBLE

You have been given permission to attend your first mixed party. Everyone is having fun watching the satellite TV until someone switches to a pay-per-view channel running an adult movie. Your friends are all laughing, but you are very uncomfortable. You know your parents will be upset if they find out.

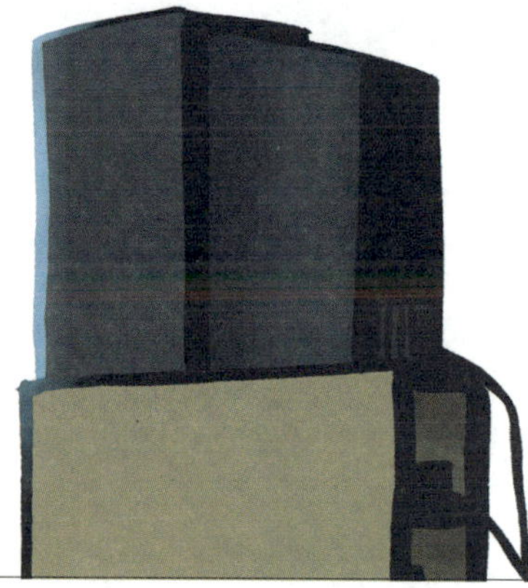

- Tell the other kids you have to go home and leave.
- Tell your friends that the movie is boring and suggest a different show to watch, or a different activity to do.
- Warn your friends about the consequences of getting caught. And tell them you don't want to lose the privilege of having mixed parties.

7 Stranger Danger

You go to the mall to meet your girlfriends Nathalie and Deqa. They have met some older guys, and Nathalie accepts an invitation to go with them for a ride in their car. Deqa thinks it's no big deal, but you are worried about Nathalie's safety.

- Take Nathalie aside and tell her she is risking her safety by going in a car with a group of older strangers.
- When someone's safety is a concern, it is important to seek help from parents or other adults. Tell Nathalie before she gets in the car that she must call her parents. And make sure she has a cellphone to call for help if she needs to.
- If Nathalie still gets in the car, immediately call for assistance.

8 Justice Buster

Your best friend Hussain had his brand-new bike stolen. He knows the guy who took it and he wants you to help him get it back. He doesn't want his parents to know because he thinks he'll get into trouble for not locking his bike up properly. You find out that the guy belongs to a gang.

- Talk to Hussain about the risks involved if you try to get the bike back yourselves.
- Sympathize with him about how hard it is to admit it to parents when you make a mistake, but encourage him to speak with his parents or another trusted adult.
- Call the police.

DID YOU KNOW?

- In Canada, young criminals used to be treated much like adults.
- That changed when Parliament passed the Juvenile Delinquents Act in 1908.

9 Broken Dreams

You are babysitting your little sister for the evening. Your parents made a deal with you that, if everything goes smoothly, you can go to the school dance. Your sister was a brat and broke your

- Hide the vase and hope your parents won't find it until after the dance.
- Without any excuses, speak with your parents calmly and openly. Admit the difficulties you had controlling your little sister and tell them about the unfortunate accident.
- Try to negotiate a fair consequence; perhaps offer to replace the vase with your allowance.

10 NOW WHAT?

Your friends are getting into a lot of trouble for breaking rules. Their choices seem to always lead them down the wrong path. And they expect you to follow.

- Talk to your friends one at a time about the choices they are making.
- Tell them about your concerns and the negative consequences they are experiencing as a result of their misconduct. Be open to hearing about the things that may be bothering them.
- Identify and discuss the positive results of following the rules.
- You may have to accept losing some or a l of these friends if their choices remain poor. No friends are worth ruining your future over.

- The Juvenile Delinquents Act was replaced by the Young Offenders Act in 1984.
- Since 2002, the Youth Criminal Justice Act has determined the legal consequences for youths who have committed crimes.
- Young persons charged with criminal offences are dealt with in Youth Court.

More **Help**

It takes time and practice to learn the skills in this book. There are many ways to deal with misconduct but only you can know which feels right in each situation. In the end, the best response is the one that keeps you safe.

If you need more information, or someone to talk to, the following resources may be of help.

Helplines

Kids Help Phone (Canada)	1-800-668-6868
Youth Crisis Hotline (USA)	1-800-448-4663

Web sites

It's My Life: http://pbskids.org/itsmylife/
KidsHealth: Kidshealth.org/kid/feeling
Kids Help Phone: http://kidshelp.sympatico.ca
Schoolnet.ca
Youthpath.ca

Books

The Breadwinner by Deborah Ellis. Groundwood Books, 2000.
Goon Squad by Michele Martin Bossley. James Lorimer & Co., 2003.
Misconduct (Sports Stories) by Beverly Scudamore. James Lorimer & Co., 2003.
Miss Little's Losers by Robert Rayner. James Lorimer & Co., 2003.
Runaway by Becky Citra. Orca Book Publishers, 2003.
Season of Rage: Hugh Burnett and the Struggle for Civil Rights by John Cooper. Tundra Books, 2005.
She Dared: True Stories of Heroines, Scoundrels, and Renegades by Ed Butts. Tundra Books, 2005.
Spud Sweetgrass by Brian Doyle. Groundwood Books, 1996.
Suspended by Robert Rayner. James Lorimer & Co., 2004.
Tiger Town by Eric Walters. Beach Holme Publishing, 2002.
The Wizzle War by Gordon Korman. Scholastic, 2003.

Other titles in the Deal With It series:

Arguing: Deal with it word by word by Elaine Slavens, illustrated by Steven Murray.
Authority: Deal with it before it deals with you by Anne Marie Aikins, illustrated by Steven Murray.
Bullying: Deal with it before push comes to shove by Elaine Slavens, illustrated by Brooke Kerrigan.
Competition: Deal with it from start to finish by Mireille Messier, illustrated by Steven Murray.
Fighting: Deal with it without coming to blows by Elaine Slavens, illustrated by Steven Murray.
Girlness: Deal with it body and soul by Diane Peters, illustrated by Steven Murray.
Gossip: Deal with it before word gets around by Catherine Rondina, illustrated by Dan Workman.
Guyness: Deal with it body and soul by Steve Pitt, illustrated by Steven Murray.
Misconduct: Deal with it without bending the rules by Anne Marie Aikins, illustrated by Steven Murray.
Peer Pressure: Deal with it without losing your cool by Elaine Slavens, illustrated by Ben Shannon.
Racism: Deal with it before it gets under your skin by Anne Marie Aikins, illustrated by Steven Murray.
Rudeness: Deal with it if you please by Catherine Rondina, illustrated by Dan Workman.

James Lorimer & Company Ltd. acknowledges the support of the Ontario Arts Council. We acknowledge the support of the Government of Canada through the Book Publishing Industry Development Program (BPIDP) for our publishing activities. We acknowledge the support of the Canada Council for the Arts for our publishing program. We acknowledge the support of the Government of Ontario through the Ontario Media Development Corporation's Ontario Book Initiative.

The Canada Council for the Arts | Le Conseil des Arts du Canada

ONTARIO ARTS COUNCIL
CONSEIL DES ARTS DE L'ONTARIO

Design: Blair Kerrigan/Glyphics

Library and Archives Canada Cataloguing in Publication

Aikins, Anne Marie
Misconduct : deal with it without bending the rules / Anne Marie Aikins ; illustrated by Steven Murray.

(Deal with it)
ISBN 1-55028-871-7

1. Etiquette for children and teenagers. 2. Conflict management — Juvenile literature. I. Murray, Steven II. Title. III. Series: Deal with it (Toronto, Ont.)

BJ1631.A34 2005 j395 C2005-900961-6

James Lorimer & Company Ltd., Publishers
35 Britain Street
Toronto, Ontario
M5A 1R7
www. lorimer.ca

Distributed in the United States by:
Orca Book Publishers
P.O. Box 468 Custer, WA
USA 98240-0468

Printed and bound in China